D0070271

The Several Tricks of Edgar Dolphin

An I CAN READ Book

THE SEVERAL TRICKS
OF EDGAR DOLPHIN

by NATHANIEL BENCHLEY

Pictures by MAMORU FUNAI

Harper & Row, Publishers • New York, Evanston, and London

THE SEVERAL TRICKS OF EDGAR DOLPHIN

Text copyright © 1970 by Nathaniel G. Benchley.
Pictures copyright © 1970 by Mamoru Funai.

All rights reserved. Printed in the United States of America. No part of this
book may be used or reproduced in any manner whatsoever without written
permission except in the case of brief quotations embodied in critical articles
and reviews. For information address Harper & Row, Publishers, Inc., 10 East
53rd Street, New York, N.Y. 10022. Published simultaneously in Canada by
Fitzhenry & Whiteside Limited, Toronto.

LIBRARY OF CONGRESS CATALOG CARD NUMBER: 79-85038
Standard Book Number 06-020467-2 (Trade Edition)
Standard Book Number 06-020468-0 (Harpercrest Edition)

For TRACY, a dolphin-lover from way back

Edgar Dolphin was young.

But he was very clever.

Even when he was small,

he could hold things in his mouth

and sometimes throw them.

7

When his mother taught him to jump,

he did it as well as she did,

but not quite so far.

Once she was teaching him
how to chase a ship.
He did it with a long piece
of seaweed in his mouth.

His mother also taught him
how to jump straight up.
After a while he learned
the right way to come down.
The first few times it hurt,
but he kept on trying.

One day he was practicing

his straight-up jumps.

He saw a strange-looking ship

in the distance.

"Well, what do you know?" he said.

"That seems interesting.

I think I'll take a closer look."

"Don't get too close,"

his mother said.

"You can't tell what it may be."

"I know what I'm doing," said Edgar.

And off he went.

When he got near, he saw

that the ship had stopped.

Funny-looking things were

jumping into the water.

"I wonder what they are," said Edgar.

"They don't look much like fish to me."

So he went a little nearer.

Suddenly, right in front of him,

there was a thing!

It had a round face

and flat flippers and was black.

"My name is Edgar," said Edgar.

"Who are you?"

But the thing only made bubbles.

"I beg your pardon?" said Edgar.

"Bobblbeeblbubbl Who?"

The thing only made more bubbles.

"I can jump straight up

in the air," Edgar said.

"Would you like to see me?"

But before he could jump,

there were more things

all around him.

They came toward him.

One had a net.

"Hey!" said Edgar.

"What kind of game is this?"

Nobody answered.

The net was slipped around him,

and he was lifted up

out of the water.

"Cut it out!" Edgar cried.

"Let me go!"

But the net rose higher in the air

and put him on the deck of the ship.

Two men laughed as they took the net.

"This is not funny,"

said Edgar crossly.

"This is either a dumb game

or a bad joke.

I want to go back to my mother!"

But the men put him into a tank.

There was water in it.

It kept him wet,

but it wasn't very deep.

"I wish I had some more water,"

he thought.

"I could jump out of here.

I suppose I could ask for more,

but these people

don't look very bright.

I doubt if they would understand."

He tried to ask for water,

but the men did not understand him.

They were very happy

to have caught a dolphin.

"Let's teach him some tricks,"

said one man.

"I hear dolphins are pretty smart."

He got a ball

and tossed it to Edgar.

"Here," he said.

"Try to catch this."

Edgar caught the ball

and threw it back.

"Good grief!" the men cried.

"He's even smarter than we thought!"

"If I had more water,

I could show you a trick or two,"

Edgar thought.

He watched one man

who was cleaning the deck

with a hose.

It began to give him an idea.

But the man was far away,

and Edgar couldn't reach the hose.

Someone threw him the ball.

Edgar threw it back,

this time with a curve.

"He's a genius!" cried the men.

"We have a super dolphin here!"

It was nice to be admired.

But Edgar was tired of the men

and their games.

He wondered when the men
would let him go.
He hoped it would be soon.
But suddenly
the ship began to move.
Edgar realized
they didn't want to let him go!

"Hey!" said Edgar.

"Let me out of here!

I want to go home!"

But the men just laughed

and thought of

new tricks to teach him.

One man tried to put

a funny hat on him.

But Edgar shook it off.

"He'll learn to like it," the man said.

"In time, we can teach him

to like anything."

"Not me, you can't!" Edgar wailed.

"I'm a dolphin.

I'm supposed to live in the ocean!

I want to go back to my mother!"

"He looks hungry," said another man.

"Somebody get him a fish."

So they got him a fish.

But before they gave it to him,

they made him throw the ball again.

Edgar was so angry that

he threw it way up in the air,

and over the side of the ship.

The men had to stop the ship

while someone was lowered

over the side to get the ball.

That made Edgar think harder.

If they wanted the ball that much,

it must be important.

Each time Edgar threw the ball,

someone jumped to catch it.

He made the men jump

anywhere he wanted,

either down the deck

or into his tank. . . .

"If I threw it

to the man with the hose . . ."

Edgar decided to wait for his chance.

Next day

when the man was

washing the deck alone,

Edgar decided to try.

He held the ball out in his mouth.

The man came to take it from him.

At almost the same instant,

Edgar THREW

the ball way down the deck,

and SNATCHED

the hose from the man,

and squirted it into his tank!

The man thought it was very funny.

First he ran to get the ball,

and then he ran to tell the others

while Edgar filled the tank.

When the men arrived,

the tank was full and

Edgar was swimming in circles.

Faster and faster he swam,

around and around,

and then he LEAPED

straight up into the air—

and over the side of the ship—

home . . .

to his mother.